# AM I A DEMON OR A VAIṢNAVA?

# STORIES *of* DEVOTION

# AM I A DEMON OR A VAISNAVA?

SATSVARUPA DASA GOSWAMI

(DRAWINGS BY ROB HEAD)

GN PRESS, INC.

PERSONS INTERESTED IN THE SUBJECT MATTER OF THIS BOOK MAY CORRESPOND WITH OUR SECRETARY:

GN PRESS, INC.
R.D. 1, BOX 837-K
PORT ROYAL, PA 17082

ISBN: 0-911233-87-3


Limited Edition: 400 copies

Cover design by Madana-mohana dāsa
and Bhakta Rob Head

# AUTHOR'S NOTE

In the Introduction to *Nimāi dāsa and the Mouse,* I justified the use of fiction in Kṛṣṇa conscious literature, as long as the Vaiṣṇava *paramparā* is kept intact, and the *"rasa,"* or devotional mood is in order. I do not want to repeat all that here, but I would like to at least ease my readers and myself into the present story. It employs fiction based on the facts of the Seventh Canto of *Śrīmad-Bhāgavatam.*

In a preface to one of his short stories, Fyodor Dostoyevsky justified his use of fantasy in a tale that is otherwise realistic. Because he raises a point that is relevant to my own audience, I would like to repeat it here. Dostoyevsky explains that his main character in "The Meek Girl" is speaking aloud in a state of shock, and the story is recorded as if a stenographer were actually present to capture his thoughts. Dostoyevsky admits that this is a fantastic element, but cites a precedent:

> Something of the same sort has been permitted in art in several occasions before: For example, Victor Hugo in his masterpiece *"Le Dernière Jour d'un Condamné"* used almost the same technique, and even though he did not make use of a stenographer, he permitted himself an even greater liberty, working on the assumption that a man who had been condemned to death would be

> able (and had the time) to make notes not only on his last day, but even in his last hour and, quite literally, at his very last moment. *Yet, if the author had not permitted this fantasy, the work itself would not exist—the most realistic and truthful work of all those to have flowed from his pen.* (Emphasis added)

My hope is that the telling of a fictional story based on the *Bhāgavatam* will allow me a freedom to convey truths of Kṛṣṇa consciousness that I would not be able to otherwise express, and also, that this form will be captivating to readers interested in the subject. If we can achieve these goals, then I think it is worth the "suspension of disbelief" that the reader must share with us—as we hear from a man named Harṣaśoka, who recorded the incidents that took place in the court of Hiraṇyakaśipu leading up to the appearance of Lord Nṛsiṁhadeva.

# CHAPTER 1

## DANGEROUS BLASPHEMY

Am I a demon or a Vaiṣṇava? That's the real question. I know the *daitya* boys are meeting in secret tonight with Prahlāda to chant the glories of Lord Viṣṇu. I should report this to their teachers, Ṣaṇḍa and Amarka, but I don't think I will.

Who do I think I am? I am Harṣaśoka, one of Hiraṇyakaśipu's clerks, right? And my son, Daityajī, is going to grow up to be an *asura* with connections to the royal family, right? Or am I wrong? Ever since my boy came home one night and started talking about Lord Viṣṇu, everything has become topsy-turvy with me. And not just with me, it is happening throughout the whole palace. Now the emperor knows too. So look sharp, Harṣaśoka, and watch your step if you'd like to keep living.

I am writing this to get my bearings. Things are going too fast, and I am afraid where they may lead. It's common, of course, for the emperor to kill someone who causes him even the slightest displeasure. I also have always believed that it is necessary to kill your enemies, or else they will kill you. For example, when Lord Hiraṇyakaśipu went to practice austerities in order to get his power of immortality, Indra and the rascal demigods immediately took advantage and ransacked the palace. So we had to fight back, and when you fight, you must kill. In order to rule over, you have to strike fear in others. I know all this and it never caused me much worry before. But now . . .

I want to get my bearings, so let me briefly describe the history up to where we are now. What came first? We won back the empire from the demigods. Everything was fine. The emperor was powerful and happy enjoying his gold and soft bed and women. And we all had plenty of the same.

The unusual events started with the emperor's son, five-year-old Prahlāda Mahārāja. The boy was always ecstatic, crying or laughing in bliss, but no one knew why. We just took it as babyish ways. Hardly anyone saw him except his mother. Since then, I have pieced together much more about him, including his extraordinary hearing of *kṛṣṇa-kathā* from Nārada Muni, while still in the womb. At that time, I knew nothing. Who was even paying attention? Suddenly, one day during the recess hour when the teachers weren't tending to the children, Prahlāda Mahārāja stood up and began preaching to them about the glories of Lord Viṣṇu and chanting Hare Kṛṣṇa! I wasn't there, but I heard it that night from my son.

It has had a strange effect on me. At first I dismissed it as nonsense, as dangerous blasphemy

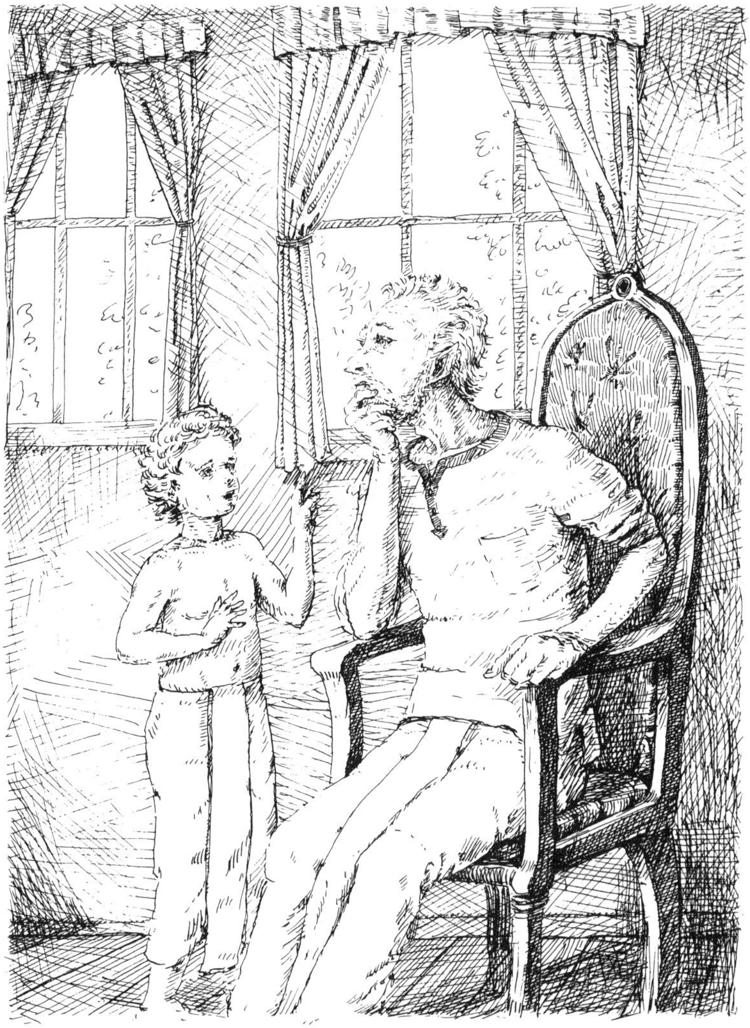

against the *asuras.* It is well known that Viṣṇu is the worshipable God of our enemies, the demigods, and that He has killed many demons who were dear to Hiraṇyakaśipu. How could the emperor's own son . . . ? But when my son explains it to me, there is something soothing and enlightening about it. Prahlāda criticizes materialistic life and exposes it as a waste of time. He says that we are not merely our physical bodies and our possessions, these things that will soon be vanquished and that give us so much anxiety when we attempt to protect them. We are not our bodies, we are eternal souls. I have heard this before and always considered it rubbish, a dream of the demigods. But Prahlāda explains it so carefully that I like hearing it from my Daityajī.

My boy looks so bright and happy as he tells me these things. He gave an example: As a geologist can tell the presence of gold in the earth and can retrieve it, so a realized sage can know the presence of the eternal soul in the body. But if you are absorbed in sex pleasure and money-making, you are disqualified from understanding the soul. Above the individual souls is the Supreme Personality of Godhead. My son said, "Being covered by the curtain of the external energy, to the atheist, He appears nonexistent." I am fascinated and have been writing down what Prahlāda tells them. I have done this for three days, and today, one of the clerks found my notebook and looked through it when I was away from my desk. "What the hell is this?" he asked. "Oh," I said coolly, "I've just been gathering some of the arguments of the enemy so that I can debate against them in a lecture I've been asked to give at the boys' school." That put him off my trail, but it is a warning that the whole affair is surcharged with danger. And I can't claim that I am unafraid.

My son taught me the Hare Kṛṣṇa mantra. I chant it in secret. All this is new to us, and I can't help myself from taking it in like a sponge. We have always been given a very limited, and I must say, distorted version of Lord Viṣṇu and His teachings. It is as if underneath my demoniac veneer, I have a natural desire to learn about spiritual life.

The boys are clever and they have managed to keep it all hidden for awhile. Ṣaṇḍa and Amarka tend to be absent-minded and they don't know what is happening. Therefore, it was the emperor who found out for himself, just yesterday, when he brought Prahlāda before him and placed him on his lap on the throne. "What is the best thing you have learned in school, my dear boy?" Hiraṇyakaśipu asked. I wasn't there, but everyone has heard what transpired. The boy began to reply nicely enough, "O best of the *asuras*, king of the demons . . . " but then he said he had learned *from his spiritual master* that the best thing was to get out of the temporary household life, which is like a dark well in which there is no water, but only suffering. One should go to Vṛndāvana, he said, where only Kṛṣṇa consciousness is prevalent, and take shelter of the Supreme Personality of Godhead.

Considering what a wild, outrageous thing Prahlāda said, Hiraṇyakaśipu acted with restraint. I have seen him kill grown men for less. He laughed and said, "Thus the intelligence of children is spoiled by the enemy." Then he gave stern orders to his assistants to protect the boy at *gurukula.* Hiraṇyakaśipu suspects that some Vaiṣṇavas are infiltrating the palace in disguise. That may be. But as far as I can see, it is only Prahlāda. He's enough to turn the whole place topsy-turvy. Even as I write this, I can't get my bearings. I don't even dare to write down what is actually in my mind and heart.

# CHAPTER 2

## SWEET MUSIC

The guards never expect anything to happen within the palace walls. After Hiraṇyakaśipu ordered them to protect the children, the guards have been extra-vigilant at the gates and parapets. Merchants and delivery men and even cleaning ladies are scrutinized more carefully to make sure that no one is a Vaiṣṇava. In fact, one mendicant was discovered who someone had previously seen wearing a *brāhmaṇa* thread and chanting a Viṣṇu mantra—and he was killed on the spot. But the palace police don't suspect that Prahlāda's "contamination" is coming from Prahlāda himself.

The boys usually play in the corridors or outside, although they stay within the palace walls. They make believe they are chopping the heads off demigods or killing cows, all sorts of games. The adults don't pay much attention to them unless they get too noisy with their demoniac screams. So nobody has noticed that they have started going apart into a grove for *iṣṭa-goṣṭhīs* with Prahlāda.

I am a bit relieved that Hiraṇyakaśipu doesn't seem to take it *that* seriously. I mean, when he gets angry, heads start to roll and it's a bloodbath. I figure that he took Prahlāda's remark about going to Vṛndāvana as mostly prattle. Also, aside from that brief exchange with his son, Hiraṇyakaśipu doesn't have further knowledge of what the boys are doing.

Most of us just follow Hiraṇyakaśipu's lead, and so the children's "Kṛṣṇa games" have not been of much concern to us either. However, it is producing a turmoil in me. I know that the boys aren't just playing games. No. Prahlāda has impressed on them that they should not waste their time playing games as they used to, but they should learn transcendental knowledge from him. He is transforming them.

By writing this down, I can see my thoughts better. I have been almost too afraid to face it. I think Prahlāda is effective with the children because they are still innocent and not yet hard-core demons, practiced to our ways. Do the other parents see this? Do other adults feel attraction to the teachings of Prahlāda as I do? I am too afraid to ask anyone. I keep silent about their "Kṛṣṇa games." Every night in private, I ask my Daityajī to tell me everything that he has learned. It's all miraculous, especially because Prahlāda is only five years old. And that's why no one suspects his potency.

*******

If any *asura* reads even this much, I'll be in trouble. So why hold back? Let me write openly and I can destroy it later.

I am happier than I have ever been in my life, thanks to the teachings of the blessed Prahlāda Mahārāja. I want to take them up in my own life, although I don't know if that's possible. I'm grateful to be able to get free of my sinful life and the karmic reactions that await me at death. By taking to Kṛṣṇa consciousness, I will not have to suffer or commit more and more abominable acts. That is, if I can give them up! Kṛṣṇa says in *Bhagavad-gītā*, "Even a little devotional service can save one from the most dangerous type of fear—the fear of falling down into the lower species." And the chanting of the holy names is so powerful that even if you chant with offenses, it can free you from sinful reaction. This is not an exaggeration.

Of course I haven't really grasped these truths, but I am hearing them and I like them very much. I have taken to reading the Vedic scriptures, which we *asuras* keep in our libraries for curiosity's sake—even Hiraṇyakaśipu knows them well—although we never let their precepts stop us from looting, killing, and engaging the senses without restraint.

But I think that now I may live my life differently. Many saintly persons started out with sinful activity and then reformed. I should think myself fortunate that I am now learning *bhakti-yoga* before it's too late. I am writing this down for my purification, but I know that I am usually still forgetful and I am still a demon. Yet a hope has arisen in my heart. The Supreme Lord knows I am just talking big empty words, but He also knows that I *do* want this spiritual life, if it is possible. What do you think? Is there hope for a demon? Can a piece of coal become scrubbed white and clean? Can a pot that has contained liquor be purified for sacred use? The sages say yes: The holy name of Viṣṇu and the association of Vaiṣṇavas is so powerful that they can counteract more sins than anyone can commit in many lifetimes.

*******

So far in this lifetime, I have lived within a firm illusion. I have always thought that I was the son of my mother and father, who were typical *rākṣasas*. We ate all kinds of flesh for dinner each night. We damned Vaiṣṇavas and killed cows and laughed at the miseries of the weak. Inside, I was a different person, but I didn't dare question who I was. One of my teachers once told me, "Don't think too much. Keep busy in life." I used to cry sometimes when I was alone, especially when I was a teenager. But then I was called downstairs for dinner, and I entered into the firm illusion.

Who am I? I don't know. I have a wife and a son. I do clerical work in the office of the emperor. I have a state identity number; I have taken the appropriate oaths as a faithful *asura*. But damn it, I don't know who I am.

Despite my bad karma, I am learning something different from Prahlāda Mahārāja. I'm learning about the *ātmā* and Paramātmā, and this knowledge is replacing the firm illusion. My son told me that Prahlāda Mahārāja said, "Dear young friends born of demons, please act in such a way that the Supreme Lord, who is beyond the conception of material knowledge, will be satisfied. Give up your demoniac nature and act without enmity or duality. Show mercy to all living entities by enlightening them in devotional service, thus becoming their well-wisher." This is like sweet music to my ears. Now if I can just learn it thoroughly and have faith. That's the crucial point: faith and trust that my soul will not die and that Lord Kṛṣṇa is the Supreme Lord and that He will protect us. I need this faith for the difficult tests ahead.

# CHAPTER 3

## DEMON OR VAIṢṆAVA?

I don't know what happened to the previous notes I wrote. Maybe they were confiscated. I haven't written anything down for two weeks, so let me focus on what has happened since then.

After Prahlāda Mahārāja made his outrageous reply to his father—that the best thing he learned from his guru was to leave material life and go to Vṛndāvana—Prahlāda's teachers tried to pacify him and pry his secrets from him. They asked him how and from whom he had learned such deviant instructions. They thought some Vaiṣṇavas may have stealthily taught him, and so they wanted their names in order to have them arrested and killed. But Prahlāda replied, as he always did, in a philosophical, compassionate way. He said, "Why do you think in terms of friends and enemies? We are all souls, loving servants of God." He was remarkably brave, you might even say foolhardy, to speak to Ṣaṇḍa and Amarka that way. But that's Prahlāda, he's fearless.

The teachers were frustrated. They said, "Oh, bring me a stick!" Since their condescending talk didn't work, they resorted to the fourth of the "four kinds of diplomacy," *argumentum ad baculum*. Then they tried drilling him with their lessons in materialistic religion, economic development, and sense gratification. After awhile, they thought he was sufficiently educated, and they tried to convince themselves that he would be all right.

Our palace is large, yet everyone knows, at least externally, what's going on. People may have different opinions, but everyone acts as if they completely agree with the party line. So what I have said so far is common knowledge. Then one day, Prahlāda's mother personally washed the boy, dressed him, and decorated him with royal ornaments, and presented him before his father. Hiraṇyakaśipu doesn't have time to play with Prahlāda on a regular basis, so these audiences, although infrequent, are significant. On this occasion, Prahlāda bowed down before his father. This touched the emperor—after all, he does have strong family feelings—so he began blessing and embracing the boy. He took Prahlāda on his lap and smelled his head. Then, with affectionate tears gliding down his cheeks onto Prahlāda's smiling face, Hiraṇyakaśipu asked him that same question, "What is the best thing you have learned from your teachers?" Of course, Hiraṇyakaśipu meant the teachers Ṣaṇḍa and Amarka, but Prahlāda wanted to tell of the best thing he had learned from his spiritual master, Nārada Muni. Prahlāda never accepted Ṣaṇḍa and Amarka as real teachers, so he didn't lie—there was nothing "best" to be learned from them.

Prahlāda said, "The best thing is . . . " and then he recited the names of the nine principles of *bhakti,* starting with hearing and chanting the holy name, form, qualities, paraphernalia, and pastimes of Lord Viṣṇu! Hiraṇyakaśipu became extremely angry. His lips trembled. He called for Ṣaṇḍa and Amarka and accused them of being heinous traitors. "What is this nonsense?!" He was ready to kill them at once. But they defended themselves, "We did not teach him this! He has learned it by himself! Do not insult *brāhmaṇas* in this way!" They had always been faithful to the throne, so Hiraṇyakaśipu accepted their version. He then directed his wrath at his little boy. He called Prahlāda "rascal" and "most fallen of our family," and he demanded, "Where did you get this knowledge?"

Prahlāda replied eloquently that it wasn't possible for Hiraṇyakaśipu to learn Kṛṣṇa consciousness because he was too sinful and he wasn't inquiring in a submissive way. He said to his father, "People like you are blind rulers leading the blind. Unless you sincerely serve a pure Vaiṣṇava, you cannot gain the education of Kṛṣṇa consciousness and become free from material contamination."

Well, that was the straw that broke the camel's back. Hiraṇyakaśipu threw Prahlāda off his lap onto the ground. His eyes were as red and angry as when he fights the demigods. "Take this boy from me!" he ordered his servants. "Kill him as soon as possible!" Hiraṇyakaśipu so much considers Lord Viṣṇu his personal enemy, that he now takes Prahlāda to be like a killer of his brother. By Hiraṇyakaśipu's logic, Prahlāda deserves to be killed.

I personally observed this exchange from a distance, along with many other *asuras* who were at court on that day. But after this, I only know what has happened to me. As for Prahlāda, I have heard only rumors. Hiraṇyakaśipu's secret police started a general purge in their attempt to find out who was corrupting Prahlāda. Anybody who is the least suspicious has been arrested. The senior clerk was interrogated and he said that I had written down some principles of *bhakti* in a notebook. Someone said that they heard me once uttering some Kṛṣṇa mantra. I wasn't asked for my explanations. I was forcibly taken from my home during dinner, the same day that Hiraṇyakaśipu gave his order to kill Prahlāda. So now I am in the dungeon. I think my son may also be undergoing punishment.

*******

Since I've been here, I've begun to repent my inclination toward Kṛṣṇa consciousness. I shouldn't have been so easily swayed by my child's infatuation for the teachings of Prahlāda. I have had many years of systematic training in skeptical philosophy, and yet I sentimentally abandoned reason and logic as soon as I heard a few precepts about

God. Maybe in another life, I might have the luxury or idleness to speculate a bit about theism. But for me in this lifetime, to risk everything in order to chant Hare Kṛṣṇa is simply not worth it.

I was thinking, "Oh, I am immortal, I don't have to be afraid even of the emperor." But where has that gotten me? If I am eternal soul—*sat-cit-ānanda* as my Daityajī told me—then why am I crying and suffering so much in this abominable hole? Why don't I just fly away on spiritual wings, or at least enter a state of happy *samādhi?* No, it's no good. All I can do is feel pain and worry about my family and wonder, "What will happen next?"

Some are meant to be demons and some are born Vaiṣṇavas. And the two always fight. It's party politics, like everything else. Hiraṇyakaśipu is right—when Lord Viṣṇu took the side of Indra against the *asuras,* it proved that Viṣṇu is not impartial. How can there be a transcendental God if He is actually partial to one warring group against another? Viṣṇu is apparently afraid and He is dependent on His allies, just as we demons are. I know the Vaiṣṇavas have counter-arguments to exonerate Lord Viṣṇu from these charges, but I don't see it just now.

Besides, if becoming a Vaiṣṇava brings such relief from suffering, then what about me? I chanted His name, I was favorable to Him, I encouraged my son, and what have I got as a result? If there is an Almighty God, He has simply kicked me in the face for no reason. How can I turn to Him now?

All the skeptical philosophers have concluded that although there is a soul, there is no supreme, happy kingdom of God. Our emperor has himself put forward good anti-Vaikuṇṭha arguments, and not without the backing of Vedic logic. After the death of his brother at the hands of Lord Viṣṇu's men, Hiraṇyakaśipu pacified his nephews with good advice. He said at that time—as we have read in the teachings of Hiraṇyakaśipu—that their father had already moved on to another life. Basically, what he taught was that everyone has to die, but that death is simply a process to get to the next life, so there is no reason to lament or fail to do worldly duties. He did not discuss the law of karma or *where* Hiraṇyākṣa had gone. He presented neither an image of a Vaikuṇṭha people went to after death, nor information about the hellish punishments awaiting a demon like Hiraṇyākṣa. He said they simply move on to another life.

Hiraṇyakaśipu can teach like that, apparently supporting the Vedic teachings. He can be quite a philosopher when he wants to be, and he knows how to use both demoniac and Vedic logic to get what he wants. In this case, he pacified his relatives in their unreasonable grief with eloquent, philosophical statements, and then he was again attentive to materialism. He mainly wanted them to get back to work. That's it.

*******

Am I a demon or a Vaiṣṇava? My roots and upbringing are demoniac. Only recently have I been dabbling in attraction to Lord Viṣṇu. I thought it would be nice to become a saintly devotee and give up sins, but it's so hard—no illicit sex, no intoxication, no meat-eating, and no gambling. The devotees make it sound so sacred and basic to give up these necessities and to strive to please Lord Viṣṇu. But who is actually doing it? Even some of the demigods break these prohibitions.

I have many questions and no reassuring answers. Where is God? Why doesn't He come to me in my hour of need? Why do people have different gods? If it's not clear who is God, then why should I commit myself to the Vaiṣṇava sect? Why defy all my authorities and friends? I can see how it would be loyal for a born Vaiṣṇava to stick to it, but why me? Why my children? And Prahlāda himself is actually a demon, but he was influenced by Nārada when he was just a helpless baby in the womb. Nārada cleverly taught him when Prahlāda was a captive audience. I can't help but think differently about it now. It's as if we have all been tricked starting with Prahlāda, and the trickster is Nārada. When I became inclined to Kṛṣṇa consciousness, I thought that it was something that I could depend on even if I got into trouble. But when you are in the dungeon, your mind gets no solace from Kṛṣṇa thought. It only makes you sorry. I fall asleep and dream and wake, and nothing makes sense.

*******

I have concluded that my interest in Kṛṣṇa consciousness is a temporary mistake and shouldn't be held against me. I called for the prison guards and asked them to let me see their supervisor. They only laughed at me. I have lost track of time. Maybe a few days ago, one of the guards handcuffed me and took me to see the warden in his office. Like the guards, he was very strongly built. He had a reddish beard and pointy teeth. A real *rākṣasa.*

"So you think you've made a mistake?" the warden asked.

"Yes," I replied, "you know my record. I've always been a loyal demon. And since being in prison, I have recovered my wits. I'm not following Kṛṣṇa! So I think I should be let out to do my normal duties again. I'm of more use to the State that way."

"Hmm. I suppose you have heard that the boy, Prahlāda, is being tortured to death."

"I haven't heard anything. I'm in the dungeon."

"Yes, yes," the warden laughed, "you are in the dungeon. So I may inform you that the boys who were corrupted by Prahlāda and who also became Vaiṣṇavas, including your son, will be punished in due course as accomplices to the villain, Prahlāda-jī."

I have been expecting as much, and have gone over such thoughts a million times in my cell. But it hurts to hear it confirmed. Being no newcomer to demonry, I could also guess why the warden was talking to me rather than letting me rot in my hole. He wasn't interested in pardons or in public relations with the prisoners.

"Yes," the warden said, "your son will be tortured and killed as soon as they are finished with Prahlāda. And then you also. It is possible that you can save yourself if you will prove your loyalty."

I nodded in agreement even before he spoke further. They want me to help find out more persons who are soft on Vaiṣṇavism. They want me to turn them in to be killed. I told them I could help. The warden dismissed me and my guard escorted me back to my cell.

It is a ray of hope, but nothing to be trusted. Not only can't I trust my fellow demons now that I had proven to them I'm a traitor, but I can no longer trust my own instincts.

Of course, I've done things like this before. As a clerk, I keep records on enemies to be killed. I used to have a high security clearance, and even know the top ten on Hiraṇyakaśipu's hit list. I have been privy to state secrets. I may not be a *kṣatriya,* but asuric blood does flow in my veins. Here is a chance at least, to try to save my life, and that of my wife and child. I'll never be restored to asuric honors, but maybe they'll let me live like an untouchable or something like that, if only I can prove myself. I wait for action. But actually, I have lost my confidence in wickedness. To tell the truth, sometimes I even wake up from fitful dreams and pray to God. Sometimes I feel some kind of inner communication or assurance from God Himself that He does exist and that he knows me. Sometimes I hear myself (or *feel* myself) chanting within, Hare Kṛṣṇa Hare Kṛṣṇa Kṛṣṇa Kṛṣṇa Hare Hare/Hare Rāma Hare Rāma Rāma Rāma Hare Hare.

# CHAPTER 4

## THE MERCY OF A VAISNAVA

I am writing again. I'll definitely destroy these pages afterwards, but it helps me when my mind is all chaos and crisis. Maybe it's my clerical training: things seem clearer when you put them into writing.

But I can't say how long it has been since I last recounted. How much time has gone by since I spoke to the warden? I thought he would call for me the next day, but no. Several times I asked the guard, but he wouldn't talk. About a week ago, the warden appeared at the door of my dismal cell. In an almost civil tone he said that there was some delay in the final execution of Prahlāda. They were still torturing him. When they decided to finally kill him, they would ask me to do that special work. More time has dragged by.

*******

A few days ago, the guards gathered about a dozen of us and brought us outside to work. We have been laying stones on top of the fortification wall.

This is where I met Tridaṇḍi. He is older than me, maybe fifty, and like me, he's frail, so they put us together mixing mortar for the wall builders. Mostly we work in silence with a guard watching us, but there are times, when the guards eat lunch or smoke, when Tridaṇḍi and I can speak. I told him that I am interred for Vaiṣṇava sympathies. He said he had been living in the mountains meditating on Viṣṇu for many years. He was naive to the boundaries and politics of our demoniac kingdom and had accidentally preached to one of Hiraṇyakaśipu's spies. He was beaten and thrown into the dungeon with us. I can still see the bruises on his face and shoulders, and there is an open sore on his arm where he was burnt. Actually, he's quite an interesting character. He's *so* thin. Sometimes when we can't talk, I find myself studying his wizened face which quickly moves from concentration to a sudden smile and then back again. Some might think he's crazy, but there is something assuring about his presence. We have been speaking to each other indirectly for the past few days, but he finally asked me, "Do you actually have Vaiṣṇava sympathies?"

"I did," I said. "But I'm ready to give them up."

"You may give up your practices of Kṛṣṇa consciousness," said Tridaṇḍi, "but Lord Kṛṣṇa will never forget you. It is stated in the *Śrīmad-Bhāgavatam* that if a person ever renders even a little sincere service, then he is never the same as other *karmīs*. Kṛṣṇa claims him." Tridaṇḍi nodded vehemently when he said this, smiled, and then nodded again.

Of course, a comment like that is forbidden. But when I heard it, it gave me a jolt. Technically speaking, I should turn him in for blasphemy, but I find myself hungry to hear more, just as when my Daityajī first came home and spoke of Prahlāda and Kṛṣṇa.

So bit by bit I am beginning to reveal my mind to Tridaṇḍi, in between mortar mixing. Some days there's no chance to talk at all, but then on other days, we are alone together for half an hour. I am beginning to regard him as an advanced Vaiṣṇava, so I am telling him my predicament.

"I don't know if I'm a demon or a Vaiṣṇava."

Tridaṇḍi replied that both the demon and the devotee often exist within the heart of a conditioned soul, where they war for supremacy.

"In my case, I am mostly a demon," I said. "The demon has the upper hand. My culture and blood are asuric."

Tridaṇḍi ran his long bony fingers through his wisp of beard, leaving flecks of mortar in it. "But according to *Bhagavad-gītā,* you are not the body; you are spirit soul. In this lifetime you may have been born in a demon family, but that's not your real identity. Take, for example, Prahlāda Mahārāja. He's the son of the greatest demon, and yet Prahlāda is the greatest Vaiṣṇava."

"Yeah, but Prahlāda is being forced to relinquish his Kṛṣṇa consciousness," I said. "In just a matter of days he will be killed."

Tridaṇḍi looked furtively over to the guards to be certain he would not be overheard. Lowering his voice he said, "That's not true. Prahlāda has actually triumphed. Hiraṇyakaśipu and his tormenters tried in every way, but they could not kill Prahlāda. They may be trying to hide this, but I know the facts. They tried throwing Prahlāda from a high cliff, but Viṣṇu saved him. They put him in boiling oil, but the boy was unharmed. He simply remained in his pure meditation on Kṛṣṇa at every moment. They put him under the feet of a ferocious elephant, but that elephant just picked him up in his trunk and put him on his back for a joyride. They tried exposing Prahlāda to severe cold and throwing stones at him, but it didn't worked. They tried administering deadly poison in his meals. Nothing harmed the boy. Hiraṇyakaśipu is completely astounded and defeated. They are afraid that Prahlāda's power is limitless. Hiraṇyakaśipu said, 'He must be immortal. In that case, I will probably die for my offenses to his master, Viṣṇu.' Prahlāda has got Hiraṇyakaśipu running scared." Tridaṇḍi chortled with glee when he said this, as if the image of a fearful Hiraṇyakaśipu was too ridiculous.

This news seems too good to be true. Maybe my Daityajī has also been spared. When I told Tridaṇḍi that I doubted what he said, he replied that I would find out for myself because soon it would become common knowledge. Prahlāda had triumphed.

*******

Tridaṇḍi speaks with such obvious sympathies for Vaiṣṇavism that I fear for his life. He told me that he usually conceals himself, but that he feels drawn to help me. When I asked about his homeland, he said he was a wanderer with no home except "back to Godhead." And he doesn't seem to be in much anxiety about his imprisonment either. He said the material body is itself an imprisonment for everyone in the world. Only when one has attained his link with Kṛṣṇa can he live freely. I am very much attracted to Tridaṇḍi's words, and even more so to his peaceful demeanor. When I contrast him with anyone else I know, I have to admit that I have never met someone so inward, centered, and self-respecting in all my life. Being with him does more to restore my faith in Vaiṣṇavism than any other possible circumstance. I think he has been sent by Kṛṣṇa to save me.

"But if Kṛṣṇa is supreme," I asked, "then why does He allow His devotees to fall into so much material suffering?"

"We must remember," said Tridaṇḍi, "that material life can never be happy. Even if Kṛṣṇa were to give a devotee all peace and prosperity in this material life, no one can live here forever. The Lord's real mercy is to somehow or other detach a devotee from all material desires, so that he can be free. And one way of detachment is to show the devotee that material life has no real pleasures and is bitter."

"Then why doesn't Kṛṣṇa at least reveal His transcendental presence to the devotee to assure Him? Since I've been in prison, I haven't been able to think of Kṛṣṇa or chant, and my demoniac nature has gotten the upper hand. I can't even defeat my own arguments that say there is no God at all."

"If you actually turn to Kṛṣṇa," said Tridaṇḍi, "you won't be lost to Him. You say that Kṛṣṇa has not appeared to you, that He has abandoned you. But how is it that both you and I have come together to talk *kṛṣṇa-kathā*, even in this horrible condition? It's Kṛṣṇa's mercy on both of us. So He has appeared in the form of our mutual *saṅga*. When He seems not to appear, we can take it as a test. Kṛṣṇa is cautious about actually giving a devotee His constant association in *bhakti-yoga* because by *bhakti*, Kṛṣṇa has to give Himself. He wants to make sure the devotee is sincere."

I am writing these questions and answers down as if they all happened at once, but it has taken weeks. I get a tremendous lift from it. Bit by bit I am getting out all the dirt and doubt. Tridaṇḍi also seems to know what's going on in the palace and he keeps me supplied with information. I can't figure out where he gets this information, but I believe what he says.

"But how do we know that Kṛṣṇa really exists? All I see are some pictures of Kṛṣṇa or some statues. Sometimes it all just seems like a myth that the Vaiṣṇavas made up. Or if there is a person Kṛṣṇa, maybe He's like Hiraṇyakaśipu says, just another big *kṣatriya,* someone who is partial to Indra." When I raise doubts like this, Tridaṇḍi sometimes chuckles to himself. Then he frowns and thinks about what I said. He always has a good reply.

Tridaṇḍi tells me what's in the *śāstras,* but he says it in his own words, with direct realization. It is coming at a time when I desperately need to hear that realization from another person and see it in his eyes. I already know some of the theoretical arguments, how Kṛṣṇa is actually impartial; how He reveals Himself only when your heart is pure; how all the great sages attest to Kṛṣṇa as the Supreme, and how many have seen Him in their hearts or had His personal *darśana.* Lord Kṛṣṇa is not partial, but He awards everyone according to their own karmic activities.

In Tridaṇḍi's presence, I find myself repeating some of the śāstric passages back to him. He doesn't really need my help, but he acts as if he does. Sometimes we feel so blissful together that we begin crying and holding each other's hands. The guards think we are lamenting our lot, but we are feeling the joys of Vaikuṇṭha and thanking the Lord. I have begun to see my physical and mental sufferings in a new light, as cleansing for my mountains of impurities and sinful deeds.

*******

Tridaṇḍi told me that Prahlāda's teachers, Ṣaṇḍa and Amarka, have requested Hiraṇyakaśipu to release the boy back into school. Hiraṇyakaśipu has become depressed about his inability to kill Prahlāda, so the teachers are trying to cheer him up. They told him that after all, Prahlāda is just a little boy. Whether he believes in God or not, what does it matter? His activities have no consequence. If Ṣaṇḍa and Amarka can just be given more time, they feel sure that they can convince the child of the excellence of the demons' materialistic teachings. They say they will teach him how to rule by diplomacy, by divide and conquer, and how to use force when necessary. Hiraṇyakaśipu has agreed. Things are as they used to be, with Prahlāda back in school. I don't know how Tridaṇḍi got all this information, but many things about him are extraordinary. Maybe he does it by some yogic power or maybe he has contacts in the outside world. But I believe him when he tells me that my own son is also no longer in prison, and that he is going to classes regularly.

*******

Yesterday I confessed to Tridaṇḍi that I made a deal with the warden to become a spy for finding Vaiṣṇavas.

"Will you turn me in?" asked Tridaṇḍi. He laughed and then frowned.

"Of course not. But what should I do?"

I know what to do. I have decided to play the role of spy, but I'll actually be counter-spy. If they ever let me out of prison, I'll live as a Vaiṣṇava. That is, I'll cover my activities as far as possible, but live to serve those who are actually partial to the Supreme Lord. I hope I get out soon. Although Tridaṇḍi's association has turned the hell into heaven, I am anxious to be with my family again.

# CHAPTER 5

## THE GUARD'S SON

The other night, the guard didn't show up with our slop-soup. His young son came. He's about Daityajī's age.

"Where's your father?"

"At war. I'm not supposed to talk to you."

The boy looks hard-faced like his father. What a miserable job it is, almost as bad as being a prisoner. But the boy is innocent. I can't help but think that he could be with Prahlāda Mahārāja and the other demon boys. But they are high-class *kṣatriyas,* and this boy is from a low caste.

"What's your name?" I asked. "You can say that much, can't you?"

"Indrajit. I'm named after Rāvaṇa's son."

"Oh, that's a big name to live up to. Are you going to become a big warrior?"

"My father says I'll be lucky to get a job outside this prison. I can't talk no more."

He pushed my bowl into the opening by using a pole, just in case I tried to leap at his hand. I wanted to tell him about Prahlāda and Kṛṣṇa, and about my son. In the back of my mind I am thinking, like every prisoner, that maybe this naive kid can be my way to escape. But I am also thinking of giving him Kṛṣṇa consciousness. I have never told any non-devotee about Kṛṣṇa before, but maybe I can preach to a young boy.

*******

Last night I told Indrajit that he reminded me of our great emperor, Hiraṇyakaśipu's son, Prahlāda Mahārāja.

"But he's a Vaiṣṇava," said Indrajit. I could barely see him standing in the corridor outside my cell, a hard-faced, unhappy boy.

"That was a misunderstanding," I said. "Now Hiraṇyakaśipu has accepted him back. He goes to school in the palace with his friends."

"What's a mis-un-der-stand-ing?" asked Indrajit. He stood as far away from me as possible, as they had taught him to do. "It's when people fight," I said. "Actually, we should all be friends because . . . everyone has the same spirit within themselves. So when we don't know this, we mistake and think that someone is our enemy."

"If you're so smart, how come you're in jail?"

I didn't exactly captivate him, but he seemed so bored and unhappy that he didn't mind lingering to talk to an interesting prisoner.

"I have a son your age who is in Prahlāda's class," I said. "I made some mistakes so I am in here. But my boy is a good *asura*. Maybe you would like to play with them. They have a lot of fun."

Indrajit looked furtively down the hall. "How could I play with the emperor's son?" he said. "I'm just prison scum."

"I could give you a note introducing you."

*******

Like my talks with Tridaṇḍi, these talks with Indrajit take place in snatches, no more than five minutes at a time. Tonight he came back just to see me; I don't know if he was authorized to do so.

"Here. You can give me a note." He pushed a pen and paper into my cell. As quickly as I could, I wrote:

> Dear Daityaji,
>
> How are you? I am well. I met a nice boy in prison named Indrajit. I thought he might be able to play with you and your friends. I can't write more now, you know. But maybe you can send me something back with Indrajit. Haribol.
>
> love,
> your Pita,
> Harṣaśoka

Indrajit read the note and then folded it into his pocket, "What does *haribol* mean?" he asked. He leaned against the far wall and looked down the hall.

"It's something you say when you feel love for someone," I said. "*Haribol* means that you bless that person. It's fun to say it between friends. If you say it to the emperor's classmates, they will like you. Say, '*Haribol prabhus!*'"

"*Haribol.*" He said it.

*******

It's been a few days since I last wrote. The day after I gave Indrajit the note, Indrajit's father resumed his duties. I was downhearted at the sight of his hard, grown-up face. I thought of saying something but didn't. But that same evening, Indrajit came to see me. Now I know he isn't coming on official duties.

"I went and played with Prahlāda," he whispered close to my cell. He was smiling and I thought that he lit up the dim corridor with his effulgence.

"Did you like it?" I asked.

"Yeah! I'm going again. Every day, if I can. My dad says it's okay since he's the emperor's son, but I didn't tell my dad what Prahlāda is doing. *Haribol!*" Indrajit pushed something into my cell with his hand, and then he ran away.

It was a letter from my son, printed in his own handwriting:

Dear Pitaji,

Please accept my humble obeisances at your feet. All glories to Narada Muni who wanders throughout the universe praising Lord Hari and who was kind to a hunter, and who is the spiritual master of Vyasadeva and Dhruva and Prahlada. All glories to Prahlada Maharaja, who showers blessings upon us in the shape of the transcendental sound, Hare Kṛṣṇa.

Mom and I were ecstatic to get a note from you and to know where you are. We are praying for you. I know you must be feeling good because you wrote "Haribol" and you induced the boy Indrajit to join our kirtana.

I have heard that it will not be long before Krsna acts, as He says in Bhagavad-gita, "paritranaya sadhunam, vinisaya ca duskrtam . . . yada yada hi dharmasya glanir bhavati bharata."

I am proud that my pita is so brave and Krsna conscious. Mom sends her love.

your affectionate son,
Daitya dasa

P.S. We have an altar now at home. This is maha-prasadam from the Deity.

> P.P.S. Prahlada Maharaja said this: "O my friends, O sons of demons, everyone including you, can revive his original, eternal spiritual life and exist forever simply by accepting the principles of bhakti-yoga."

The *mahā-prasādam* was a morsel of dried *halavā.* I knew it would be blissful, so I didn't gulp it. I worshiped it first. My prison practice has been to imagine opulent offerings for the Deity, but since it is all done in my mind, sometimes the offering suddenly disappears and I can't get back to it. I will be preparing sweet rice in one pot and steaming *sabjī* in another pot, when suddenly my mind goes to some past demoniac scene, eating meat or laughing at Vaiṣṇavas and so on. Or I just space out and the offering gets forgotten. And as for the daily slop they bring us, it's hard to "honor" it. Still, I do it. I thank Kṛṣṇa for providing us the *bhakti* method whereby we can give Him our devotion with prayers when we eat. I recite the Sanskrit and then I say to Kṛṣṇa that I know we would be eating lumps of sin if we didn't offer the foodstuff with prayers. I ask Him to let the prayers be more important to me than the sense gratification of eating afterwards, and I ask to be able to *honor* the *prasādam.*

I have taken only a pinch of the *halavā* and I'm saving the rest. Suffice to say the *halavā prasādam* is one of the best things I've ever tasted, and it was just a tiny pinch. *Mahā-prasādam-sevā kī jaya!*

*******

Indrajit came to see me again in the early evening. He sat on the floor just outside my cell and spoke in a soft voice. He is particularly impressed by Hiraṇyakaśipu's palace, which he has never entered before.

"The steps is made of coral," he said, "is that whattcha call it? There's them bright green things all over the floor and the walls are real shiny. The people're all decked out in fancy silks, even the boys. They even got gold bracelets and stuff."

"So the boys are your friends now?" I asked. "Did you see Prahlāda Mahārāja?"

"Yeah! He was dancin' with his arms raised up. He had a flower garland with roses in it. He was singin' and we all danced round him. I never seen demon boys like that!"

"Did you talk with them?"

"Yeah, but I mostly listened. I ain't able to understand so good. But I like dancin' and singin' Hare Kṛṣṇa. And they gave me some food. Hey, Mr. Harṣaśoka, what's an *ātmā?"*

There are usually a few bars of sunlight filtering down to the dungeon, and at night it grows dark. In the almost total darkness, I told Indrajit about the *ātmā,* the spirit self. Then he asked about Paramātmā. I told him he had a good memory for the words. Paramātmā, I said, is the supreme soul from whom everything comes. And He kindly resides in each person's heart to guide us. We have to turn to Him.

"Can ya do it even down in this rat hole?" he asked.

"I try."

"And what's a *śāstras?*" Indrajit asked.

"The holy books given by Bhagavān, the Supreme Person. They are perfect, not like the books an ordinary person writes. We can learn everything from *śāstra.*"

"What's the difference between demons and devotees?"

"There is no difference in spirit. Both are sons or daughters of Bhagavān. But demons don't obey the Lord. Devotees obey Him. Like you and me, we are demons according to the bodies and families we belong to, but if we act as devotees, then we are no longer demons."

"What is eke-wa-poised."

"When you don't get disturbed even in a bad place. When you see all people equally. Only one who knows the Paramātmā in all persons can be equipoised."

Kṛṣṇa has rewarded me with *prasādam,* and now with preaching to Indrajit. I am not able to preach to the big guys, but this pint-sized demon is the right size for me, a perfect recipient. Thank you, Lord Kṛṣṇa, thank you, Prahlāda Mahārāja, and thank you, Daityajī for bringing home the teachings of Nārada Muni to your covered-over father.

*******

Indrajit has continued to visit for the past three nights. He brought me a small piece of silk which he said was a piece of Prahlāda Mahārāja's *cādar*. Another note from my son and my wife. Another morsel of *prasādam*. And more earnest questions about things he has heard directly from Prahlāda but doesn't understand.

"Hey, Mr. Harṣaśoka, what's it mean when Prahlāda says, 'O sons of the demons, your duty is to take to Kṛṣṇa consciousness, which can burn the seeds of fruitive activities?'"

"The seed means our material desires. Say you burn down a field of dry grass. It will grow up again next season. So if you stop the horrible acts of the *asuras*, that's good, but later you will do them again unless you take out the 'seeds' and burn them. Kṛṣṇa consciousness can do it."

"What is the *ka-la-ca-kra?*"

"Time is like a wheel, Indrajit. It rolls over us and cuts us to pieces, and kills all our gains of a lifetime. Even Hiraṇyakaśipu will be destroyed by the *kala-cakra*. And after one life, we have to take another life according to our karma, and again in that life, we lose everything at death. It's an endlessly rolling cycle, like a wheel, *kala-cakra*."

Indrajit and I always speak as quietly as possible, but one of the prisoners overheard us. He called out in the dark, "Knock off that shit."

"Indrajit," I whispered. "I hope you never forget these lessons of Prahlāda Mahārāja. I hope you take them to heart. Be careful and protect them as your most valuable possession."

"Yeah. I'll do it, Mr. Harṣaśoka. I gotta go now. *Haribol*."

The next day when Indrajit's father passed by my cell, he said that his son wouldn't be coming to see me anymore. "I know he's been sneakin' in here," he said, "but someone complained. So no more." The guard figures it is good for his son to mix with the boys in the palace, but he knows Prahlāda's position is uncertain, and he's wary. But I doubt that he knows how much has transpired between myself and his hard-faced little son.

So another promising relationship has ended. How soon all the relationships of a lifetime will come to an end! Kṛṣṇa save me and protect me!

# CHAPTER 6

## HIRANYAKASIPU'S POWER

Has it been weeks or months since I last saw Tridaṇḍi? I met him again during an unusual assembly called by the prison authorities for all inmates. They gathered us into the yard where military leaders and prison wardens addressed us about the possibilities of an all-out war with the demigods. In the event of an empire-wide emergency, prisoners will be expected to bear arms against the invaders. Whoever discharges such duty honorably will get his freedom. It is typical asuric rhetoric, about how Indra is afraid of Hiraṇyakaśipu, and how we *rākṣasas* are the best race of people and have nothing to fear. But just in case . . .

Tridaṇḍi appeared beside me, smiled, and said into my ear, "This rotten regime won't last long."

I turned my head cautiously and asked, "How do you know?" I spoke as low as possible in hopes that I would hear something encouraging from him before they noticed us.

"It is predicted by sages and seers," said Tridaṇḍi. "All the planetary leaders have been very distressed by Hiraṇyakaśipu, and at last they have surrendered to the Supreme Personality of Godhead, Viṣṇu." Tridaṇḍi said the word "Viṣṇu" with emphatic devotion, but I cringed, thinking he had said the name too loudly.

"They worshiped Him in deep meditation," said Tridaṇḍi, "especially by meditating on Him in the direction of the holy *dhāmas.* And then they heard a transcendental sound vibration. The voice was as grave as the sound of a cloud and very encouraging, driving away all fear." He widened his eyes and smiled, seemingly unaware that we were surrounded on all sides by *rākṣasas,* prisoners as well as big-shot leaders. I wanted to ask Tridaṇḍi, "Where did you hear all this?" But there was no time for curious inquiries.

"What did the Voice say?" I asked. "Make it short."

"The Voice of the Lord," said Tridaṇḍi, "said, 'Do not fear, become My devotees by hearing and chanting and offering Me prayers. I know all about the activities of Hiraṇyakaśipu and I shall surely stop them very soon. Please wait patiently. When Hiraṇyakaśipu teases the great devotee, Prahlāda, I shall kill him immediately, despite the benedictions of Brahmā."

"Shut up over there!" A guard had heard speaking from our ranks, although he didn't see exactly who had spoken. A prisoner shoved Tridaṇḍi in the ribs. He stood straight and looked forward, but I had already heard enough.

At the end of the military chief's speech, he shouted, "So, are you demons ready to fight for your freedom?"

"Yeah!" they yelled in a furious uproar of assent, although mutters of "bullshit" were also heard.

"Then wait for the moment," said the chief. "We do not know when they may come, whether in the morning or at night, but at that time, we will unite to push back the agents of Indra, and even if Viṣṇu Himself dares to come, He will be destroyed!"

As we were herded back into our cells, it seemed to me that the prisoners were unimpressed and unchanged by the speeches, except that we were all excited by the general assembly and the departure from routine. For myself, I feel lighthearted and confident, ready to endure austerities, because I believe in the words of Tridaṇḍi. The whole universe is suffering from the fever of meningitis due to Hiraṇyakaśipu, but soon, his terror reign will be removed.

Later that day, while I was still floating on a cloud of confidence and well-being, the guard said he was taking me to see the warden. Despite our silent sharing of knowledge about Indrajit, the guard never says anything friendly or civil to me. But as he handcuffed me and pushed me ahead with his spear, I couldn't help but express my feelings.

"Don't worry," I said, "your son is in good hands. We will all be delivered by the emperor's blessed son."

"Shut up!" he said. "No more lip."

*******

I gave all my previous notes to Indrajit to give to my son. But these present notes I will destroy. I can tell it all only in part and briefly . . .

In my mind I call the warden "Copperbeard." To his face I say, "Sir." He called me to discuss my assignment of spying on the Vaiṣṇavas.

"I know more about you than you think," he said, "and I am doubtful whether you will actually cooperate."

He seemed pitiful in his make-show of power, with his sword and cudgel, big biceps, and the brass bell on his desk in case he needs more help. I thought of Prahlāda's teachings, how the *mūḍhās* think they can protect themselves, but we conditioned souls are all under the powerful grip of *māyā* and time.

"The emperor has decided to cure Prahlāda by education," said the warden. "But he also said once that his boy was like the curved tail of a dog—he cannot be straightened. We are all awaiting further orders from His Majesty."

I am beginning to wonder how much the secret police actually know. Do they think that Ṣaṇḍa and Amarka have the situation under control? I am in solitary confinement and yet I have managed to

learn that Prahlāda is actively teaching and leading the sons of demons in *kīrtanas*.

"We need someone trusted both by the boys and their families to gather information. But can we trust you, Harṣaśoka?"

Copperbeard is a hundred percent duplicity, so talking with him is always a cat and mouse game. But on this occasion, I felt less tight. I had just heard about the voice of Viṣṇu assuring the demigods that Hiraṇyakaśipu would soon be smashed. I dared to hint at it.

"Who knows, your honor," I said, "how long all this will last?" I said it with a little smile. (Now that I recall this, I think I was playing the philosopher, being proud.)

"What do you mean?" He pierced me with a demanding look.

"I mean that all our affairs are governed by time and destiny. Whether we spy or not, no one can escape his karma."

"Oh, really?" Copperbeard pushed himself back in his chair, matching my smile with his own. "Tell me more," he said.

"I can't tell you." I wasn't *all* pride. I was earnest too. I know it was foolhardy. My heart was thumping loudly, but something was impelling me to say it.

"You can't understand," I said. "But even the emperor's power and life duration are limited compared to the forces of eternal time. We are all subjects of the same supreme force, but one of us acts as a warden and one of us acts as a prisoner."

That was as far as I got. He slammed his fist down and screamed, "Shut up, fool!" Then he stood up and put his hand on the bell. "Don't you understand?" he said. "I could kill you in a minute. I don't even have to explain it to my authorities. You are just like an insect to me."

I knew he could do it. I feared for my life. After that, I lost my bearings, lost my grip on transcendental knowledge. I was cringing and all inside myself. But it was too late to play cagey.

"Let me educate *you,*" said the warden, "on the power of Lord Hiraṇyakaśipu."

I had not only angered him, but I had insulted his pride. He readied himself for a patriotic speech, as if to clear the air from my insolent remarks.

"Hiraṇyakaśipu has gained immortality," said the warden. "He earned this by performing incredible austerities, never before undertaken by any living being. He has been promised with all the binding force of Lord Brahmā, that he can be killed neither by day or night, nor by any manmade weapon, nor on land or sea. There is no beast that can kill him. In other words, he is immortal. Although Brahmā claimed that he himself is not immortal, Hiraṇyakaśipu outsmarted him and got the benediction he wanted."

As with everyone else in the kingdom of Hiraṇyakaśipu, I have already heard this a million times. But I no longer believe it.

"As a result of this benediction, and because of his great personal prowess, Hiraṇyakaśipu is seeking to revenge himself against Lord Viṣṇu, who killed his brother, Hiraṇyākṣa. You should have learned all this in your early school days. Did you not?"

"Yes sir, I heard it as a boy."

"But you have forgotten. So learn it again. Our lord has virtually taken control of all the three worlds. We are in fact, at this moment, occupying Indra's seat and his palace. Everyone pays tribute to Hiraṇyakaśipu. For example, the inhabitants of Pitṛloka now offer their *śraddhā* ceremonies only to Lord Hiraṇyakaśipu. The proud inhabitants of Siddhaloka have had their powers taken away and Hiraṇyakaśipu is now the single and greatest mystic. Our lord has also taken away the meditative power of the inhabitants of Vidhyādharaloka. He has forced them to abandon their meditation by of his superior bodily strength. He has also taken away the wives and the jewels of the inhabitants of Nāgaloka. He has destroyed the *varṇāśrama* system by breaking the backs of the Manus. He has forbidden the *prajāpatis* to create anymore good progeny. He no longer allows the inhabitants of Gandharvaloka to dance and sing for their Viṣṇu, but they are now under our lord's subjugation. In short, he has subjugated everyone. Even the famous Nārada Muni, who likes to travel here and there singing foolish songs about Viṣṇu, is no longer seen in these parts. Or perhaps you have seen him?"

"No sir, I have not," I replied. And so it went.

The warden said that he would be "merciful" to me and not kill me this time. At least not immediately. But he would think of some measures for my punishment and reform.

*******

Now it's a few days after my interview with the warden. I'm back in my cell and my *sādhana* routine.

I have no "solution" to this fear. It did teach me a lesson, however. I plunged so quickly from the heights of fearlessness down to the depths of fear. I see that I am not ready to master even the first lesson of *Bhagavad-gītā:* "I am not this body; I am spirit soul."

It is embarrassing to my self-esteem. For a few moments in the warden's office, I acted like a dauntless devotee-follower of Prahlāda Mahārāja, but when that demon was ready to kill me, I cringed.

I don't want to dwell on it here. I am just trying to get my bearings. At least I don't believe a word of what they say of Hiraṇyakaśipu's immortality. I'm sure his day of defeat will come, and before too long, as stated by the voice of Lord Viṣṇu. We all hope that it will be soon! Therefore, just because the warden frightened *me,* doesn't mean that he proved Hiraṇyakaśipu is more powerful than Time or Fate. And Time and Fate are expansions of the expansions of the Supreme Person.

Lord Viṣṇu is great, and Hiraṇyakaśipu is, by comparison, less than an ant. That will soon be proven. But *I* have also been proven to be an insignificant and fearful person. My body consciousness is more prominent than my God consciousness.

But I am dependent on You, Lord. If I do something shameful under torture, if they force me to denounce You, please forgive me. Don't reject me. Know that I am Your weak servant. If they say, "Give us the names of Vaiṣṇavas," I pray, please let me die in Your service.

Since I am cowardly, let me not philosophize on fear. But with my limited faith and devotion, I will chant Your holy names. Yes, *that* has increased—the fear has prompted me to bow down to You more often and to utter Your names feelingly. I am afraid of *māyā.* I am afraid of death. I worship You, Lord Viṣṇu, protector and friend of the most fallen.

# CHAPTER 7

## FOR THE LORD'S PLEASURE

By Kṛṣṇa's grace, I am writing this from outside prison. It has been two days since I escaped. In some ways, the present situation is just as intense and oppressive as prison. So I am noting it down—what has happened and what I am supposed to do now.

Indrajit came in the middle of the night to my cell. He said he wanted to run away from home and join Prahlāda's classmates. He had the guard's keys to free me. As quickly as that, I was out of my cell. I asked him if we could free Tridaṇḍi also, so we went to his cell. At first, Tridaṇḍi shrugged and waved a bony hand at us, but we convinced him that he might be killed here and that he could practice his *bhajana* better elsewhere. While discussing this, we almost got caught. The night guard walked over our way and we quickly hid in Tridaṇḍi's cell. The guard flashed his torch into the cell, but saw only old Tridaṇḍi sitting erect in his lotus *āsana*.

"Damn fool, be quiet," the guard said. "No talkin' out loud."

When the guard passed, the three of us ran out into the night, past all the walls and into the city lanes.

"I'm heading for the mountains," said Tridaṇḍi. "I want to pray for the appearance of the Lord." I stopped for a second to watch the thin form of my *yogī* friend disappear into the darkness, then turned to face Indrajit.

I wanted to see my family. "Indrajit, come with me," I said. "We'll find a safe place for you."

So I went home and woke up Daityajī and my wife. It was a wonderful reunion but I couldn't stay there more than a few minutes. As soon as the police discovered me missing, they would come to my house. Daityajī said he knew a place where I could hide. So here I am. It's above a baker's shop. All over the country Vaiṣṇavas are in hiding. Some are in caves and some, like me, are in attics or basement cubbyholes. There is a network of sympathizers giving shelter to persecuted devotees. But the police keep looking and sometimes finding.

The baker is keeping me here at great risk to himself. I hate to put him into jeopardy. I have to be even quieter than in my cell. My *japa* is strictly silent. I can't even cough during the day or walk on the floorboards.

But I can read again. The Vaiṣṇava scriptures are here. And I am in touch with the world.

The biggest immediate problem is Indrajit.

*I wanted to be a devotee and Kṛṣṇa is giving me the chance.*

Almost as soon as I arrived here I began to write. I don't mean this narration about myself. I have started to write an essay proving that the Supreme Lord is equal to everyone. This is one of the arguments the demons use somewhat persuasively over fellow *asuras*. They say that Viṣṇu is partial to the demigods and so He is not supreme. With the scriptures available for reference, I am able to make cogent arguments against this demoniac interpretation and express it in my people's daily language. I can't wait to talk with Daityajī about the possibility of getting an essay printed secretly and distributing it among the *rākṣasas*. It's a way for me to render service and to preach. Otherwise, what good is my training in reading and writing, unless I can use it for devotional service?

I am halfway through this essay, but I've thought of two more that I could do. One could be on the theme that although you may be born and raised as a demon, you can become a devotee of Viṣṇu. I should be able to convey that. Smash the *asuras*.

I am bold with my plans for the pen, but actually I am afraid. We are all afraid under Hiraṇyakaśipu. But me especially. All right, but I can do this, write against the demons. I can sit quieter than a mouse up here, not squeaking the floorboards, and write. I must do it. It's bliss. And if in the end I get caught, well, at least I have attempted something. That's what human life is for. Now, let me get back to my essays.

*******

Indrajit is a great problem. He wants to go home again. I have just spent three hours talking to him to convince him that he's done the right thing in surrendering to Kṛṣṇa. But what can you expect? He's only nine years old. He needs his father and mother. What to do? He knows if he goes home, they will kill him or he will have to tell them that he freed me. What's done is done. Somehow, the boy had an inspiration to run away and to become a devotee, but now he's losing heart. I know what that's like. And it's so hard here, having to remain so still and silent. He freed me from prison only to feel imprisoned himself. I'm trying to be like a father to him, but I'm not an effulgent devotee. I have begged him to wait until the morning when Daityajī is coming. If only the Supreme Lord would appear, then everyone would be free.

*******

The boys have moved Indrajit to a hiding place close to their school where he is always in the association of some of the classmates. He is happier there, I hear. He doesn't want to go back to his father and the prison routine anymore. The boys around Prahlāda Mahārāja are like beautiful moons around the sun. The whole community of *daitya* boys are becoming Kṛṣṇa conscious. My own son is like a ray of Viṣṇu. And I'm not just saying it because I'm his father. Rather, as Tridaṇḍi said, Daityajī is more like my spiritual master. As soon as he came here—was it two days ago?—Indrajit's spirits immediately picked up. My boy is like a touchstone. And a staunch devotee. He is picking up my spirits too.

*******

Daityajī has been explaining to me that pure devotional service is unmotivated, done just to please Lord Kṛṣṇa. I see that I have been praying with a wrong conception of spiritual life and the spiritual world. At heart, I have been seeking a peaceful place within the material world. Even my concept of going back to Godhead has been to attain a place where there are no chained bodies or foul smells or cold, a place free of cruel guards and no Hiraṇyakaśipu. It's natural, I suppose, to desire this, and to speak of it to the Supreme Lord while I chant His names. But in the spiritual world (and in the heart of the pure devotee) the concentration is on devotion to the Lord and pleasing Him. The spiritual world is, therefore, not a place where everything is perfectly adjusted to my tastes—my favorite music and food and climate and aesthetics—but Goloka is the place where everyone serves and loves the Supreme Lord, and everyone is fully satisfied and delighted in that.

In this material world, there can never be peace. Don't absorb yourself in approaching Kṛṣṇa and asking for it—"Please protect my body, my honor, my family." He can do it as a favor or reward for my service, but ultimately, nothing can endure in this world. If my whole heart is absorbed in that fruitive desire for personal well-being, even well-being within a devotee's life, then that will replace my intention to please Lord Kṛṣṇa. This is a subtle point, and yet it's very basic. I have been selfish and fearfully seeking protection, but what I seek is a temporary shelter.

Let me just write it down here one more time so that I can look at what I am saying: A pure devotee is pleased only because of the Lord's pleasure. The Lord is pleased to see the devotee engaged in devotional service. Even if there is unhappiness in terms of material conditions, if the devotee is faithfully serving Kṛṣṇa, then he sees even those impediments—prison, lack of facilities, lack of any protectors or maintainers, being bereft of friends, punished, etc.—he sees all this unhappiness as a kind of happiness. Because he is trying simply to serve Kṛṣṇa, therefore he sees beyond the happiness and unhappiness—to the pure bliss of only depending on the Lord and asking to serve Him. If this pure state of being is as yet unattainable for me, at least I must always remind myself that this is the goal. Association with pure devotees and hearing from the scriptures will help me. If my prayer is,

"Please Lord, give me peace, free me from the hands of the demons"—then I will miss the goal. Now I understand better why it didn't matter to Tridaṇḍi Prabhu whether he was freed from prison or not. He wasn't sure whether Kṛṣṇa wanted it.

*******

Daityajī has printed my essay, "The Supreme Lord is Equal to Everyone," and they are passing it around. Some demons aren't so schooled in asuric philosophy; they are ignorant and they serve in fear. It won't cost them so much effort or be so risky to read a pamphlet, and maybe it can turn them. I was turned, so why not others?

Now I am working on a pamphlet about the Supreme Lord's appearance in the world. Tridaṇḍi and other devotees know of signs that indicate that Lord Viṣṇu is going to appear very soon. I can't write about that so much because I don't have definite information. But I will write on the basic principle that the Supreme Lord is concerned with this world (although He is aloof from its laws of karma). He does come to the world, as stated in *Bhagavad-gītā,* whenever there is a decline in religion and a rise in irreligion. I want to encourage people, whether they are demigods or demons, with the reminder from scripture that the Lord will appear and is already here in His name and teachings, and in the form of His pure devotees.

People are oppressed and looking for relief. "Why doesn't God come to rescue us?" Well, we should know for certain that Kṛṣṇa is acting—personally, in the form of His son or servant, and sometimes Himself in a disguised form.

I am not writing as an empowered prophet, but I am ringing the temple bell, so to speak, to wake people up by saying, "He's coming, the Lord is coming. Be patient, the king of the demons will soon be killed."

In the meantime, we may be killed by Hiraṇyakaśipu for speaking out in this way. But it is service and the Lord expects it. The *avatāra* will come whether or not we distribute a pamphlet, but when He comes, it will be of crucial importance for individuals whether they are His devotees or think of themselves as enemies of the Vaiṣṇavas.

Prahlāda's classmates gave out some pamphlets at a wrestling match by placing them in the seats of the stadium. The authorities found them and were ripping them up, but many people hid their copies. Then there was some graffiti written under a bridge, "Demons, give up hatred of the Supreme!" and "Chant the names of God," which may have come from the pamphlets. The boys have been meeting receptive people—people who aren't interested enough to read scriptures, but who are willing to talk with them about Viṣṇu.

*******

Daityajī has the notes I sent with Indrajit from prison. I read them and I was surprised at how much I was swinging back and forth like a wild pendulum. "Am I a demon or a Vaiṣṇava?" Actually, I'm just a pretender. It would be a joke if I were to claim, "Now I'm a Vaiṣṇava." Between the two identities, I am probably still more of a demon, or I'm an ex-demon maybe. I don't know who I am. But my dear Lord, I know that I wish to be Your devotee. If I am a demon by past habits or thoughts, by my blood and karma, etc., at least I'm not *acting* as an *asura.* I can attest to your mercy on us demons. I am thankful for my new life. Like a typical nondevotee, I still think fearfully, "What will happen next? What will happen next?" But at least now I worry within the context of a devotee's life. Please give me the strength to serve You.

# CHAPTER 8

## THE LORD SLAYS THE KING OF THE DEMONS

The boys are alarmed. Ṣaṇḍa and Amarka, dull as they are, have finally discovered what is going on. All the students, the sons of demons, are becoming advanced Kṛṣṇa conscious devotees because of the association of Prahlāda. It's like the entire youth of the ruling class, the elite, are already Vaiṣṇavas. Ṣaṇḍa and Amarka are afraid, no doubt for their own necks, but also because they hate devotees. They were so puffed-up and blind, they thought that by teaching Prahlāda speculation and materialism, it would replace his attachment for Lord Viṣṇu. Not only did they fail to change Prahlāda, but he has deeply convinced all the other boys to follow his instructions. They *are* still children who like to play and run and joke, yet they are also becoming wise, compassionate transcendentalists. You have to see it to believe it. It blasts your previous conceptions that a child must be selfish and completely attached to sense gratification. Not these boys. Although it's already too late, Ṣaṇḍa and Amarka are afraid that Prahlāda's influence will spread even further. They are going to report this to Hiraṇyakaśipu.

This happened just this morning. It may mean a crackdown on Prahlāda and our boys. When Hiraṇyakaśipu concentrates his attention on someone as an enemy, it is murder. Maybe he will also look for people in hiding like me.

*******

I saw some military officers approaching the baker's building. They entered and I heard them talking below. Within a couple of minutes the baker came upstairs and said, "They're coming up. Hide in the dog house." So I did, gathering up my books and papers. The "dog house" is a small crawl space. The baker threw a padlock on it once I got inside, in hopes that that would prevent them from going further. Then they came up and started talking about how the room looked suitable for the government's purpose, so they would use it. They wanted to place a big table in there for laying out blueprints. Two of them went away, but one of them stayed. And so I was trapped in the dog house.

There is an opening where I can crawl out on to the rafters, but that would make too much noise. I know that I can't hold out long in this cramped position. At least there is some light coming from cracks in the roof.

I wonder, "How can I please the Lord here?" I recall Daityajī saying that instead of praying for one's own safekeeping, devotional service really means to think about and execute services that will please the Lord and His devotees. I know one service I can perform is to stay calm. And because I am prodding myself to do some service, I am imagining it.

I imagine many persecuted Vaiṣṇavas getting together in a remote part of the forests or mountains and starting an army. There is a camp with some tents and wooden lean-tos, and a concealed campfire. I have a prominent role. I am in a tent talking to some of the leading devotees, but what am I doing? Many young boys are up here and I am taking care of them. I am educating them. I am a more advanced devotee and teaching them philosophy. I am trustworthy. Some big leaders find comfort in talking with me. I forage for wild vegetables in the forest and practice austerities in an exemplary way. We prepare for the revolution, or for the advent of the Lord . . .

The *rākṣasa* who so suddenly invaded my room is now snoring.

Maybe daydreaming is not service in itself. At any rate, the main thing is not to see myself as some wonderful person of my imagination—I should think of doing something *actually pleasing* to Kṛṣṇa.

Instead of thinking of myself as a devotee, I am trying to think of Kṛṣṇa's pastimes. I remember Daityajī telling me about the behavior of Prahlāda Mahārāja and how he is so ecstatic. Prahlāda sometimes sits, and just by thinking of Kṛṣṇa, he starts to cry profuse tears. Sometimes he laughs and sometimes he sings or cries out in joy. He sees the Supreme Personality of Godhead in his meditation and calls out loudly in devotional anxiety. Daityajī said that sometimes Prahlāda has seen the Lord coming from a long distance to pacify him, like a mother responding to a child saying, "My dear child, do not cry. I am coming." Then Prahlāda begins dancing and thinks, "Here is my Lord! My Lord is coming!" Sometimes he is in full ecstasy and imitates the pastimes of the Lord, just as the cowherd boys used to imitate the behavior of the jungle animals.

*******

I haven't finished my quota of rounds today. At least that is something appealing to my mind. If anything else, I am dutiful. Silently chant the Hare Kṛṣṇa mantra and count off the quota on my fingers. The day is turning to dusk.

*******

I awoke to a tumultuous sound. I have never heard such a loud and commanding sound in my life. Rather than try to describe it here, I can better say what it *feels* like. There is a tremendous sound of thunder. I am afraid. There is something supernatural about it, something insistent. My hairs are standing on end. This sound is like a hundred thunders and it hasn't stopped. It seems to be cracking the covering of the entire sky. I'm sure everyone else, like me, thinks that the planet is being destroyed. Is it a bomb? An earthquake?

There, I've crawled along the ceiling beam to the edge of the roof. There are big cracks in the tile and I can see outside. Although it's night, the sky is filled with light. Clouds are scattered here and there. *Rākṣasa* airplanes are being thrown up into outer space as if from an explosion. But there is no smoke, no fire, just light. From my perch I can see the agitated sea foaming. The hills seem to be *growing*, but at the same time, the earth seems to be slipping down. At first I was thinking it was an earthquake, but it doesn't add up. The light is unearthly. It diminishes the stars and the moon.

People are running in the street completely dazed and looking around for the origin of the sound. Everyone is terrified. Elephants are screaming.

I am praying by saying the Lord's names. If this is the end, then let me die while chanting and thinking of Kṛṣṇa. Surely Kṛṣṇa is behind this wonderful tumultuous sound and light. Will we all be destroyed? *Kṛṣṇa!*

The baker just unbolted the closet door and called me. "What's happening?" I asked.

"Someone says the palace is being attacked," he said. We hear the palace sirens ringing, although they are puny compared to The Sound. The militia and police and special combat soldiers are racing to the palace. From the direction of the palace, although it is a few miles away, we can hear screams and the sound of clashing weapons.

I said, "Let's sit down and chant, what else can we do?" A few Vaiṣṇava friends are arriving and we are all prepared to chant Hare Kṛṣṇa until our last breaths. We are still afraid of Hiraṇyakaśipu, so we have turned off the lights. But there doesn't seem to be any reason to be shy anymore about calling out the holy names. We aren't thinking straight, but at least we are together, uttering His names, Hare Kṛṣṇa Hare Kṛṣṇa Kṛṣṇa Kṛṣṇa Hare Hare/Hare Rāma Hare Rāma Rāma Rāma Hare Hare.

As we chant, the sky continues to scintillate with a beautiful light, and the earth is filled with tremors. The thunderous Roar holds us in awe.

*******

Not much time has passed but suddenly the atmosphere has changed. The Roaring continues, but it is slightly subdued. From all directions, there is now a palpable sensation of relief. We devotees are looking at each other because we can all instantly feel it and recognize it. Something very auspicious must have happened. Up to this point, the streets have been filled with shouts and military orders. Rumors were flying fast as to what was actually happening. Everything was completely contradictory and confusing. Someone said that the demigods were being destroyed, and others said that the demons were vanquished. But now everything feels certain and peaceful.

One of the young boys said, "Kṛṣṇa must have come. Hiraṇyakaśipu is dead."

Still, we're not so brave as to wander out. We are keeping our places. The chanting of Hare Kṛṣṇa remains appropriate. With increased strength and with many of us displaying bodily symptoms of ecstasy, our little group goes on calling, Hare Kṛṣṇa Hare Kṛṣṇa Kṛṣṇa Kṛṣṇa Hare Hare/Hare Rāma Hare Rāma Rāma Rāma Hare Hare.

*******

Daityajī just burst into the room! He is still breathless from running, but he looks completely sanctified, transformed into a Vaikuṇṭha being. But it's my son!

"I saw it!" Tears are streaming from his eyes and I know they are the cool tears of transcendental joy.

"With His claw . . . " Daityajī said and made a claw with his tiny hand and fingernails. "I saw His

claw! His nails . . . He tore out the king of demon's intestines and put them around His neck! . . . "

He went on to tell us what he saw and partially realized. It has since been told by many eye witnesses, and has been expressed in choice poetic language by the great sages as Vedic *śāstra*. We were on the outskirts and also saw wondrous things that have never been seen before. By the grace of Prahlāda Mahārāja, my son was present to see the appearance of Lord Nṛsiṁhadeva, who killed the king of demons and then sat on his throne.

*tava kara-kamala-vare nakham adbhuta-śṛṅgaṁ*
*dalita-hiraṇyakaśipu-tanu-bhṛṅgam*
*keśava dhṛta-narahari-rūpa jaya jagadīśa hare*
*jaya jagadīśa hare*
*jaya jagadīśa hare*

# EPILOGUE

I cannot assess what happened on that glorious night. Now, like every other devotee, I read about it in the *śāstras* and understand it in that way. For example, we all know that after the demise of Hiraṇyakaśipu, Lord Nṛsiṁhadeva remained very angry and roaring. Even the great demigods could not pacify Him. But on the request of Lord Brahmā, Prahlāda Mahārāja went forward and fell at the feet of the half-man, half-lion incarnation. Lord Nṛsiṁhadeva was ecstatically pleased to see His devotee Prahlāda, and he patted him on the head. Prahlāda Mahārāja then spoke sublime prayers to pacify the Lord.

Dear readers, you too may hear the complete prayers of Prahlāda Mahārāja as recorded in *Śrīmad-Bhāgavatam*. But I would like to note down here two of the statements of Prahlāda Mahārāja to Nṛsiṁhadeva. These were most impressive to me and to others who heard them related, and who began to talk of them constantly in the days that followed.

Prahlāda Mahārāja said that he had no qualifications to approach the Lord, especially when other demigods were not able to do so. But he said that the Supreme Lord is not particularly pleased by any material or religious accomplishments other than pure and humble devotion. I never tire of hearing how our beloved Prahlāda said to the Supreme Lord, "Although I was born in a demoniac family, I may, without a doubt, offer prayers to the Lord with full endeavor, as full as my intelligence allows. Anyone who has been forced by ignorance to enter the material world may be purified of material life if he offers prayers to the Lord and hears the Lord's glories."

In other words, Prahlāda Mahārāja paved the way for all ex-demons. Prahlāda is a *mahā-bhāgavata,* but he is "one of us" because he appeared in a family of demons.

We were also impressed that Prahlāda Mahārāja gave all credit to his spiritual master, Nārada Muni. Although Prahlāda was approaching the Supreme Lord directly, it was only by the mercy of his spiritual master.

Prahlāda took the occasion to remind all materialists that opulence and enjoyment are all unworthy pursuits. He said, "When my father was angry and he laughed sarcastically at the demigods, they were immediately vanquished simply by seeing the movement of his eyebrows. Yet my father, who was so powerful, has now been vanquished by You within a moment."

And may we never forget Prahlāda's prayer to deliver all the *mūḍhās* and rascals unto the lotus feet of Kṛṣṇa. Prahlāda said that he did not even want to go back to Godhead unless he could bring with him all the bewildered conditioned souls. As followers of Prahlāda Mahārāja, we shall also not go alone and seek only our own spiritual salvation. But we will go door to door to try to convince people that without taking shelter of Kṛṣṇa's lotus feet, one cannot be happy.

Lord Nṛsiṁha wanted Prahlāda to take a benediction. The Lord was very touched at heart that Prahlāda had undergone so much suffering. But Prahlāda replied that he did not want to be tempted by having to think of rewards. Whatever he had done as service to the Lord was done in love and from the constitutional nature of the eternal servant on behalf of the Supreme Master. But when Lord Nṛsiṁhadeva insisted, Prahlāda asked for the benediction that his sinful father, Hiraṇyakaśipu, could be spared from sinful reactions. The Lord replied that this request had already been fulfilled.

We are all happy living in this world under the protection of Prahlāda Mahārāja. Lord Nṛsiṁhadeva told him, "It does not matter that you are in the material world. You should always, continuously, hear the instructions and messages given by Me and always be absorbed in thought of Me. I am the Supersoul existing in the core of everyone's heart."

I too now have a part to play within the kingdom of Prahlāda Mahārāja. I gained his personal audience and he has given me duties to perform and emphasized *śravanaṁ-kīrtanaṁ viṣṇoḥ smaraṇam*. There are still impediments due to the residue of past desires, but gradually, I am feeling more cleansed. Never for a moment do I vacillate between being a demon or a servant of the Vaiṣṇavas. In this life and in future lives, I am determined to remain a loving servant of Lord Kṛṣṇa, and I pray that the same may be true for whoever reads these words.

I would like to thank the following disciples and friends who helped produce and print this book: Bhakta Rob Head, Caitanya-rūpa-devī dāsī, and Kaiśorī-devī dāsī

## Other Books by Satsvarūpa dāsa Goswami

*Readings in Vedic Literature*
*A Handbook for Kṛṣṇa Consciousness*
*He Lives Forever*
*Śrīla Prabhupāda-līlāmṛta (Vols. 1-6)*
*Distribute Books, Distribute Books, Distribute Books*
*The Twenty-six Qualities of a Devotee/*
*Vaiṣṇava Behavior*
*With Śrīla Prabhupāda in the Early Days: A Memoir (formerly titled: Letters From Śrīla Prabhupāda)*
*Japa Reform Notebook*
*The Voices of Surrender and Other Poems*
*Remembering Śrīla Prabhupāda (Vols. 1-5)*
*Remembering Śrīla Prabhupāda (1 Volume)*
*Life With the Perfect Master*
*In Praise of the Mahājanas and Other Poems*
*Prabhupāda Nectar (Vols. 1-5)*
*Living With the Scriptures*
*Reading Reform Notebook*
*The Worshipable Deity and Other Poems*
*Under the Banyan Tree*
*Dust of Vṛndāvana*
*Journal and Poems (Books 1-3)*
*Guru Reform Notebook*

*(other books cont.)*

*Prabhupāda-līlā*

*Pictures From the Bhagavad-gītā As It Is and Other Poems*

*Lessons From the Road (Vols. 1-17)*

*Iṣṭa-goṣṭhī (Vols. 1-3)*

*Nimāi dāsa and the Mouse: A Fable*

*Nimāi's Detour*

*Gurudeva and Nimāi: Struggling for Survival*

*Choṭa's Way*

*Truthfulness, The Last Leg of Religion*

*Prabhupāda Meditations (Vols. 1-4)*

*Prabhupāda Appreciation*

*ISKCON in the 1970s: Diaries*

*Memory in the Service of Kṛṣṇa*

*Obstacles on the Path of Devotional Service*

*Talking Freely With My Lords*

*Viṣṇu-rāta Vijaya*

*Śrī Caitanya-dayā*

*My Search Through Books*

*Shack Notes*

*Here Is Śrīla Prabhupāda*

*Begging For the Nectar of the Holy Name*